Quiet Geography

Michael C. Keith

Červená Barva Press
Somerville, Massachusetts

Červená Barva Press
P.O. Box 440357
W. Somerville, MA 02144-3222

www.cervenabarvapress.com

Bookstore: www.thelostbookshelf.com

Cover art: "Winter Cove" by Richard Hoffman

Cover design: William J. Kelle

ISBN: 978-1-950063-74-1

Library of Congress Control Number: 2022938709

TABLE OF CONTENTS

ABOUT THE AUTHOR

Quiet Geography

It's just indigestion. Thanks for asking.
                    —Ian Rankin

*I can talk for a long time only when it's about
something boring*
                    —Lydia Davis

To take my work seriously would be the height of folly.
                    —Edward Gorey

Frontier Priorities

She was left alone in the cabin while her father went to check the traps. He told her he'd be back before sunset and they'd have fresh meat to eat for supper. Now, the sun had long since set and her father had not returned. What bothered her most was not having fresh meat to eat for supper.

Do Bhaile

Fiona and Maisie were cousins and very fond of one another. The only tension existing between the two arose from their defensiveness about where they lived. Each thought the home of the other inferior to theirs. Maisie had lived in Cumbernaud her whole life while Fiona had called Glenrothes home for over a decade. The conflict was finally resolved to their questionable satisfaction when both communities were recognized with the Plook on the Plinth Award for the most dismal town in Scotland.

His Late Friend

He'd just been phoned by a friend and told a friend had died when he noticed a text from the friend who he was just told had died. He wondered if he had seen the message first and then ignored the call, if he'd still be waiting at Starbucks for his friend, who he'd just been told had died?

Observed the Sannyasi . . .

"The fact there is always a popular new war movie reveals much about human nature."

Shut Eye

He believes he's come up with a viable plan to defeat his insomnia. One night he takes 10 mg of Melatonin. The next night two-thirds of a cannabis gummy. The third night .25 mg of Xanax. The fourth night 5 mg of Melatonin and 200 mg of Ibuprofen. The fifth night 250 mg of Tylenol PM. He begins the cycle again on the sixth night. With this approach, he gets to sleep shortly after turning in. Tonight, however, his thoughts have overtaken this strategy.

Tangles of Comfrey, Cranesbill, and Spurge

As conscientiously as McDougall gardened, the results betrayed him.

Continuity Error

The movie critic called the film depicting life at a remote ranch in the sun-scorched desert of 1890s southern Arizona flawless, except for the lush green salad served to the cowpokes in their dusty and airless bunkhouse. "How did it happen they had fresh garden veggies in that parched desolation?" he inquired.

Out on a Limb

The last time Chelsea walked in the field next to her cottage she saw a humanlike shadow move across its side door. It startled her and she figured it must have been created by the bright moonlight and wind rustling the branches of the pine tree that stood a few feet from the house. The next evening as she took her postprandial she saw the silhouette again and was startled by the thought it resembled her recently deceased husband. When she turned to look at the nearby evergreen, she spotted him perched on a branch. "Oh, my dearest," she said. "Come down from there before you break your neck again."

Gazette Obit

MYERS, Frederick C. Age 82, of Maplewood, was a veteran who served with distinction at home during the war. He was a heavy smoker and imbiber of alcoholic beverages. He is survived by his cat, Ovid.

Stalin Makes Lunch

Joseph's babushka Geladze had a special way to prepare Golubtsi. As a boy, it was his favorite dish. He had not made it himself since becoming Russia's premier but following the Central Committee meeting in which a member voiced respectful opposition to his plan to improve sanitation in the Kremlin bathrooms, he felt a renewed urge to cook and share the cabbage dish with that particular individual. He varied the recipe only slightly, making a small adjustment to its ingredients.

End-Life Goal

Shana was losing interest in the things that had always engaged her. Soon she wouldn't care about anything, and she'd be fully prepared to face the end. It had taken her 86 years to get to that point, and it hadn't been easy. She felt a sense of accomplishment, aware not everybody achieved a state of total indifference.

Considerate

I eat applesauce from a cup with my finger. I do it alone so as
not to offend anyone, because eating food with your finger is
not condoned in polite society.

Making a Meal for Melissa Was Uncomplicated

She was very fond of chickpea soup. In fact, it was her favorite food. This was well known among her family and friends, who would serve her chickpea soup whenever she came to their house for lunch or supper. "Thank you very much for serving me chickpea soup," she would say, with genuine gratitude. "As you know, it is my favorite food."

Post Literate Damage

I find I'm reading much less and spending more time on the Internet. I worry about that because I hear screen time does not stimulate the brain the way the printed page does. Already, I sense my intellect has dulled because I'm coming up with fewer answers watching "Jeopardy."

Distressed

If you don't mind, let me fill you in on what's going on with me right now. Maybe after I do you'd give me your take on it? I could use some perspective, because I feel I'm losing it. On the edge, as they say. So, then, here goes. For the last three days, I've noticed a 1940s model two-door sedan with green side molding at several of the places I've been. At first, I was intrigued, because I love vintage cars, but when I kept seeing it, I began to wonder what was going on. Was I being followed, and, if so, why? It never got close enough for me to see who was inside. Then this morning I'm watching an old video of downtown Cleveland on YouTube and a car just like the one I've been seeing, green stripes and all, pulls in front of the camera. Now, I can see through the driver's side window and it's me . . . *me!* I've never even been to Cleveland.

Going Where the Muse Takes You

I write a paragraph but it isn't right. It fails to convey what I intended. After studying it, I decide to scrap it and start again. This time it's nowhere near what I originally wanted, but I like it better.

Getting to Know You

The recently arrived Tethysian wanted to know if it was doing okay with its human gestures and mannerisms. It was part of its acclimation training program. As an instructor, I was told to never say anything negative during these sessions because the extraterrestrials didn't take well to criticism. However, on this one occasion, I forgot the rule and said I thought it needed to work on its handshake. That thrusting out its razor-sharp, sword-like appendage was not the best way to greet the inhabitants of my planet. To my relief it kept its cool and even helped me bury the two Earthlings with whom it had just attempted to shake hands.

White Lie

The lilac bush against our driveway has popped. I'm allergic to its flowers, or so I think, but my wife adores them. I tell her my running over it was an accident. That the turn I made was too wide.

Michael C. Keith

The Man Who Almost Hit Stephen King

Every time the famous horrormeister published a new novel, which seemed almost weekly, Jeremy was reminded of how close he came to running him over. He'd seen him walking the quiet country road near his home a number of times and had even exchanged waves with him, but two days before the author was actually hit by Bryan Smith, he'd come close to plowing into him. He'd nodded off for a split-second because of fatigue—too many third shifts at the mill for extra bucks. King had not seen him swerve from the road in his direction and as soon as he was out of the writer's sight, he stopped and shook out the cobwebs, his heart in his throat. *What the hell was Smith's life like after the accident?* he wondered. *Did King get revenge casting him in one of his books? A drug overdose maybe?*

Recognizing the Value in What's Around You

The best day of Frank's life on his off-grid spread in the high desert of southern Arizona was when he realized there was a fortune to be made in Mesquite beans.

"Do It Right for Less"

A dollar fifty-nine was what Home Deport charged for a pair of latex palm coated work gloves. Chad didn't think there was a better bargain to be had anywhere. *Less than two bucks to protect your hands? Are you kidding?* he thought. He needed to thank somebody and asked to see the store manager.

The Odds

"What is the likelihood I'll return in human form if I'm reincarnated?" asked the acolyte.

"About one in 10 million," replied the prophet, adding, "Far more likely you'll return as a deer tick."

Blame Game

He cuts his fingers putting metal plaques on bowling trophies. It's the only job he can get after graduating from high school. He comes to hate bowlers, even though he knows none. *Why would they do this to me?* he huffs, thinking he may go to Paradise Lanes after work and confront a league with his bloody wounds.

All but the Essential

Bernice was smart, considerably above average. But there was one area in which her high intelligence did not benefit her. It was knowing when best to cross a busy street. That deficiency cost her.

Pushing the Limits of Transportation

The 1972 Tiffany Edition Oldsmobile Ninety-Eight Regency Sedan with Rocket V8 engine was everything he ever wanted in a luxury vehicle. In a letter to General Motors he expressed his profound appreciation for its commitment to craftsmanship. He believed when American enterprise excelled, it should be told so.

Family Avocations

His dad collected guns, new ones mainly. His mom gathered what she called "Depression-era" glass. When they were with their stuff, they didn't scream at each other. He figured he needed a hobby, too, to keep from screaming.

Young at Heart

Katlyn remembers her mom saying she couldn't believe she was 80, because she still felt like a kid. It was her birthday and you could understand why she would say that because she was so vibrant and full of life. She passed away two years later due to a newly prescribed blood thinner which caused her to hemorrhage internally. Even in youth, there are no guarantees.

Sue's-chef

His wife refers to the nightly meals he makes as beige buffets.
They lack suitable color for her taste.

Ghost Writer

He'd worked for four years on his latest novel and the only thing reviewers and readers wanted to talk about was its ending, which had been proclaimed as one of the most brilliant and memorable in contemporary American fiction. "Where did that come from, Scott?" inquired his close friend and fellow writer. "I'm not saying the rest of the book isn't good but, my god, that last paragraph should be enshrined in the literature hall of fame. It's absolutely transcendent." Scott nodded in feigned appreciation but thought he'd go off the deep end if he heard that one more time. Why did his wife have to pencil in the ending when he'd gone on a quick errand? Yes, he'd complained about having a tough time completing the last chapter, but did she have to finish it for him . . . and so damn brilliantly?

Pride and Prejudice

A pickup truck with white nationalist flags waving from its cargo bed cruises down our street. It upsets my mother-in-law. "Why don't they take their patriotism somewhere else?" she asks.

Between Earth and Muleshoe

It wasn't a dozen miles either way from where the couple had been born, but to hear her husband talk about it she may as well have bought the house lot on the moon. His attitude about living between the two small west Texas towns changed when he heard a P. Terry's was going to be built a half mile from their future residence. The convenient access to his favorite fast food restaurant transformed his thinking. "Okay, I can do that," he announced, quelling the tension between the long-married Lone Star staters.

Belief

He wanted irrefutable proof of the existence of ghosts and then he would return to church with a whole new attitude.

Not Disney World

The Millers took the Supratour bus ride across the Sahara to Merzouga. The family of five slept the entire trip, and when they arrived at their destination 12 hours later, they wanted to take a camel ride. After being told all the rides were booked for the day, they decided to return to Fez immediately, figuring they'd seen what was worth seeing of the desert.

Telegram from Ex-Pat

Summer '29 STOP Jimmy behind bar at Falstaff STOP Asks what I want STOP Tell him Absinthe STOP Second since coming to Paris STOP Can't get it back in States STOP I'll stay here STOP

Working Toward a Resolution

He found a black wavy hair under his egg in the diner where he ate. It disgusted him to find a black wavy hair under his egg. He waved the waitress over and showed her the black wavy hair under his egg. She said "Did you put the black wavy hair under the egg to get a free breakfast?" This incensed him, and he picked up the plate with the black wavy hair under the egg and tossed it. The waitress retrieved the plate with the black wavy hair under the egg and returned it to her customer, declaring there was no longer a black wavy hair under the egg.

Disappointment

Cyril believed if he published his manuscript, he wouldn't mind dying. He'd accept his end contentedly, but once his novel published, he realized that thought, too, was a fiction.

Michael C. Keith

Streets of Dreams

When he came to, he found himself sitting on a bench next to a towering stone edifice. An unfamiliar flag flapped in the breeze on a pole above him. He had no idea where he was or how he got there. He rose and walked to the corner of a street named Selari. There he took a left onto Francesa. Then a right onto Postei and followed it to Lipscani until it reached Smardan. By then he sensed he wasn't in Kansas anymore.

39

Advice

"You must be careful in this life. It's so easy to get into trouble. To ruin yourself in the eyes of others. Look at James, for instance. He pushed so hard to get noticed, and look how he's regarded now."

From a Lecture by the Professor of Thanatology

"It was common in the old days to lay out the deceased in the home, often on the kitchen or dining room table. At meal time the family of the recently departed would set plates and silverware around the corpse, placing condiments on it if space was tight. This was especially the case if the dead person's body was large. Of course, this would sometimes result in relishes and sauces falling to the floor."

Guest Hosts

Alex in an urn and the game goes on.

A Carefully Orchestrated Plan

My friend asked me to take care of her dog while she went on vacation and I agreed. She knew I was an animal lover and had recently lost a pet of my own to old age. Her dog was very loving and easy to take care of, and I fell in love with him. The idea I'd have to return him to my friend when she returned from vacation bothered me greatly, so I thought of a way I could keep him. I put him in a kennel and when my friend got home I said her dog had gotten loose and had not been found. Of course, she was upset, but she understood things like that happened. A week later when my friend stopped coming around, I brought her dog home from the kennel. It all worked out rather nicely.

Anne, Sylvia, Virginia . . .

From their smiles in old photographs you got the impression
these were women who would not hurt themselves.

Other Worlds in the Bathroom Floor

Every time he sat on the toilet he noticed something different in the new flooring. He'd been studying the linoleum since it was installed and discovered it contained an infinite variety of images and scenes, which kept him engaged for long stretches of time. "When are you going to be finished in there?" inquired his wife. "As soon as they release me from their spaceship," he answered. "Oh . . . okay, hon, I'll use the downstairs john," she replied. She'd been abducted by aliens herself in the upstairs bathroom.

Sleeping Rough

Esther was found dead in a Four Penny Coffin and thus was buried without further expense. There was, after all, an advantage to being sick and poor in Victorian London.

Last Kiss

He was choking and the only living thing near him to which he could appeal for help was his dog. He made a desperate grunt that brought his pet to his side. One last loud gasp and the pooch lovingly licked his blue face. For a moment, he was saved.

Upmanship

Archie had been a lighterman on the Thames for 37 years until his arthritis forced him to retire. He felt great pride in his career despite his younger brother's frequent contention he, as a waterman, held a higher place in the social pecking order of river workers since he conveyed people rather than goods.

It Was Enough to Convert the Dedicated Bachelor

She was unlike any woman he'd ever met. Yes, conventional in most ways, but she could levitate. A proposal was forthcoming.

Celtic Cowboy

After watching *The Broncho Kid* with Hoot Gibson at the Louxor Cinema in Paris, literary icon James Joyce told his former publisher, Sylvia Beach, he was thinking about writing a western featuring Stephen Daedalus as an Arizona sheriff hunting cattle rustlers with his Navajo sidekick, Shem. She suggested he finish his newest Dublin-based novel first, even though she'd been having difficulty getting through the early draft.

Quiet Geography

"Do you know how many broken hearts there are in Talmage, Kansas?" asks the old woman gazing at the giant grain elevator across from her house. "Not a damn one."

The Speed of Technology

We're walking with another couple today. They do Fitbits so want to get in as many steps as possible. They think to do this they should walk really fast. We like to keep a decent pace, but sometimes walking with them feels like an Olympic event. Later, we tell them they're moving too quickly for us to enjoy the outing. We say we think their Fitbits are the problem. They acknowledge our suspicion, and say they won't use them the next time we get together. That was a year and a half ago.

Butterfly Wings

He was a Consequentialist. Consequently, he would not leave his storm shelter for fear of the consequences.

Bedside Manner

"As you age, your mind does begin to slip," said Jonah's gerontologist when he complained of having difficulty recalling things and engaging in the everyday activities of the world around him. "It's called senescence, but 76 isn't old-old. However, it's certainly the point when humans are no longer as sharp as they once were. Bet you have a bunch of aches and pains, too. Look, Jonah, you need to learn to accept where you are at this late stage in your life and not fret over it. Doing that will only accelerate your disintegration and speed up the atrophying process. It's a downhill spiral now, so my best advice is to enjoy your golden years before they run out."

She Was Wise to a Point

He's doing everything in his power to annoy me, but I know the thing that annoys me the most, and I'm not going to tell him . . . unless he stops annoying me.

#NotMeToo

His coworker claimed he'd sexually abused her. It had never happened, and he didn't know what to do to convince people otherwise. Once accused, innocence didn't matter. The world would always suspect you were guilty regardless of the facts. So, he thought he may as well live up to the charges against him and waited for her in the underground parking garage.

An Oversight

What they hated most about autumn was the falling leaves. It was not the raking but how they left the trees naked, exposing the nuclear power plant abutting their property. They regretted buying the place during the summer.

A Foreign Remedy

I was hold-up in a hotel in Arusha with a sick stomach. Something I'd eaten the day before on the ride up from Dar es Salaam had laid me low. While I was resting, there was a knock on my room door. I figured it was the tour guide checking in on me, but to my surprise two attractive scantily-clad young women greeted me. "We wish to know if you would like us to make you feel better," they inquired. We had pharmacy delivery back home in Connecticut but Tanzania had clearly taken that service to a whole new level.

Last Wish

He hoped to spend his final moments alive gazing at the nighttime sky. Its mystery suggested infinite possibilities and gave him hope his existence might somehow continue. His challenge was to avoid dying during the day.

Looking Ridiculous in Front of Your Pet

My dog and I communicate in a fully conscious and intelligent way—not just human to animal and vice versa. I look in her eyes and she looks in mine and there's a powerful exchange of thoughts and ideas. She is as bright as any person I know. "What do I do with that information?" I ask, and she responds, "Oh, for God's sake, Brian . . ."

When All You Have Are Lemons . . .

Severe drought compounded by two winters of record breaking freezes created the perfect storm for the majestic blue spruce trees gracing the quad of northern Iowa's Central College. It was the worst case of Cytospora Canker arborist Howey Ferguson had ever seen. "Can they be saved?" asked the college's distressed president, who knew all too well that without the magnificent conifers the campus would look like a strip mall. "No sir, they're dead already. Nothing you can do but dig them up and dispose of them, I'm afraid. You could cut off the branches and leave the 100 foot trunks in place. Of course, that would look pretty strange" That afternoon the school's printing office was directed to prepare flyers announcing the institution's forthcoming outdoor exhibit of post-apocalyptic art.

Phantom Limb

When he was beheaded he could feel his entire body for seven seconds.

The Forgotten Mistakes of History

When Callum Mulreach remarked that tearing down the ancient Clovelly mills to build an Amazon fulfillment center would prove as regrettable in the future as the demolition of the Stones of O'on, his fellow protesters quickly Googled his obscure reference on their cellphones. Several gasps ensued.

Rest Stop

He came across an image of his father's grave on Google and took a photo. He hadn't visited it in 20 years. *This is a good way to avoid the drive*, he thought.

A Renewed Interest in Life

Mabel could find little to be happy about. She was old, childless, poor, and unattractive (no-one is really attractive in their 80s, she surmised). Thus, she found herself deeply depressed as soon as she woke up and remained that way throughout the day. Finally, she decided to end it. To put a stop to her despair by no longer taking her life-sustaining meds. She figured not having to choke down 25 pills a day would, in itself, improve the quality of her existence. This notion gave her mood a significant boost and when weeks passed with no dramatic side-effects, she began to suspect her doctors had been conspiring against her. *Okay, let's see what I can do about that*, she thought, looking through her undies drawer for her deceased husband's Glock.

Withholding

He alone had discovered the answer to the age-old question of how life came to be. After thinking about revealing what he knew to his fellow humans, he decided it would just take too much effort.

Dirty Old Professor

She was the most devastatingly beautiful young women he'd ever encountered, and she was his student advisee. He clearly hadn't concealed his arousal at seeing her because a look of discomfort immediately replaced the 19-year-old's smile as she sat before him to discuss her course schedule. He tried not to stare, but he couldn't help himself. She held his interest with a totality he'd rarely experienced. After handing her the audit sheet she needed to register, he asked if she had any questions. "No," she answered, and made a hasty retreat. To his disappointment, it was the last time he saw her, and he later learned she'd switched advisors. In the year that followed, he enjoyed countless erotic fantasies wherein she was the central figure. *How would she have reacted if I hadn't been 80 . . . maybe 60 and had hair?* he asked himself.

A Change Was Comin'

I saw a video from back in the 60s of one of the greatest protest singers of all time. I'm glad he finally got his teeth fixed.

Price of Glory

On his daily commute from Silver Spring to Foggy Bottom via DC's Metro, Oscar sees "Cool Disco Dan" scrawled across countless buildings, billboards, and bridges. He wonders how vain someone has to be to write his name all over public objects. He considers if he can get away with it, too.

Achieving Serenity

"When I woke up I felt as peaceful as I had the last time. It was that special kind of peace. The kind you get after you've shot someone you don't like."

How Is It Some People Confront Fate with a Smile?

His first novel was a bestseller and made him a lot of money. With his newfound fortune, he decided to move to The Isle of Sky, a place he always fancied. As his bank account swelled, he contacted a realtor in Portree and found the home of his dreams. He quickly sold his small house in a suburb of Glasgow, and relocated. It wasn't much later he was diagnosed with a terminal disease. *Well, that was a bloody good three months,* he told himself.

Child Care

Clarence was not born happy and remained tearful through his childhood. His parents were grateful to have found a way to quell his endless weeping for a few moments. It took their son that long to recover his breath after being punched in the stomach.

Adventure Tourism

We visit Joe's Flamingo Jungle in southern Florida. A safari van painted in camouflage takes us into the park's dark recesses to where we're told the exotic birds typically congregate—no explanation offered as to why. The location is on the rim of a gelatinous body of water overhung by palmetto palms and moss trees. The tour guide directs our attention to a cluster of the vibrant pink creatures on the far shore. My father huffs and then grumbles as he looks through his binoculars. When we return to the visitor's center my mom asks why he was griping, and he reports half the flamingos were plastic.

A Writer Calls a Fellow Writer with a Question

"Do you remember how at the end of his show Red Skelton would say "God bless?" I've been trying to figure out how to convey the unique way he said it but I'm not nailing it. Any suggestions?"

What's Your Sequence?

My wife asks, "What routine do you use when you wash your body in the shower?" I'm puzzled by her question and ask what she means. "What part of your body do you wash first and what do you wash next? What's the last thing you wash?" I think about it and answer. "My hair. Then I work my way down," I say. "Down to where?" she inquires straight-faced. "My toes," I mutter, growing irritated by her odd line of questioning. "You're very weird," I blurt. "If I'm weird, you're dirty," she replies, adding, "Do you know how many parts of your body you miss?"

The Young Romantic

He reflected back to the time he felt compelled to carry his would-be lover, no matter how heavy, to his bed like John Wayne did Maureen O'Hara in *McLintock*.

Things Are Figured Out Over Time

Raoul was having a snake fence installed. Rattlers were fond of using his stone patio to sun themselves. If the diamondback hadn't devoured his old Chihuahua, Asenino, he wouldn't have bothered. The culebras weren't bad to look at, kind of beautiful in their own way, but chowing on his best friend turned him against them, especially when he figured out you couldn't train one as a house pet.

14 November

I see my father's date of birth mentioned on page two of *Tropic of Cancer*. Out of 365 days in the year, what is the likelihood of that? It can't be just a coincidence, I figure, and wonder how well my father knew Henry Miller.

I Will Not Pretend Everything is Rosy

My wife is tired of what she calls my negative attitude, and I know she's not alone. I can't help it because everything seems so bad to me. The world is crumbling under all the cruelty and terrible leadership. Every morning I get up wondering what horrible thing has happened overnight. What new misery have people inflicted on one another? Every observation I make is based in fact, so I shouldn't be condemned for telling it like it is. I advise those who criticize me for my so-called doom and gloom view to go ahead and cure the ills of humanity and then I'll be more positive. They think it's just more of my being negative when I say that.

The Overly Friendly French

Of all the zinc bars in Paris, he favored *Les Papilles* on *Rue Gay-Lussac*. There he was able to drink undisturbed. He'd found it was not easy to enjoy one's own company without interruption in the city's other cafes. Then the day arrived when a patron of *Les Papilles* insisted on conversing with him. It was at that moment he decided to return to Des Moines.

Scene at the Vets

A boy emerges from an animal hospital clutching a box and weeping. His mother asks if he'd like to go to Wendy's in an obvious attempt to raise his spirits. He looks at her through tears and brightens. "Okay," he says.

81

Image Issue

He accidentally sent his buddy a heart emoji instead of a thumbs-up. This prompted a response that gave him pause. To wit:

"Thank you, my dear friend, I feel great affection for you, too, and I'm glad to lend you my power tool anytime you need it."

Michael C. Keith

Answers Often Raise More Questions

When I asked what will become of me after I die, the oracle replied, "You will be bound and gagged and locked away in a fourth-floor garret in 1936 Stockholm after your sudden death in 2041."

Past Glory

I recall the point in my career I felt validated because I'd written a journal article that drew positive comments from fellow scholars, some noted. I now look back on the piece with a sense of failure because of the important points it failed to make. I wonder if those who had such good things to say about it would now be embarrassed by their lack of insight?

Staying the Course

Now that Sheila was closing in on the end her life, she was suddenly aware she'd always seen things from a negative perspective. *Big deal,* she thought.

Upon Reconsidering

Okay, he said, when I said I would do all the cooking from now on after he complained of having to make the meals all the time. You'll have to do the laundry if I'm doing all the cooking, I told him. Well, I really don't mind doing all the cooking, he said.

Close Call

When she heard him climb the stairs to their bedroom before she was up, she knew why. "Spread 'em, baby," he said, approaching her, hand rubbing his crotch. "Why do you say that? Not very romantic," she mumbled, half awake. "Uh oh, not in the mood, eh? Okay, see you downstairs," he replied, dejectedly. *That was close*, she thought, pulling the blanket over her head.

Mom on What Would Be Her 97th

Less and less is said of her absence.
No cake, no presents, no birthday song.

Poor Me

Three days after his book had been nominated for a prestigious award, the marketing person at his publishing house died in a freak accident while on a celebratory mini-vacation in Ocean City, Maryland. Her support for his work had been extraordinary, so her sudden death in a freak accident shook him. He believed nothing worse could happen and then his novel failed to win the coveted prize. *Life just hasn't been fair to me*, he told himself, bitterly.

Mislabeled

When Noah was little he didn't understand why people called the building he lived in a ghetto since only one black family lived there.

Thankful He's an Accountant

He watches the famous astronaut and thinks wistfully that could have been him. Moments later, he sighs in relief because the famous astronaut he could have been is trapped in a spacecraft spiraling out of control on the other side of Uranus.

Routine

Burl's route took him from Davenport, Iowa, to Omaha, Nebraska, and then back to his home base. A 600-mile loop in all. About 10 hours driving with a one hour layover in Omaha to swap buses for the return leg of his daily run. As a Trailways employee, he made the trip four times a week and had done so for 22 years. He believed his job was a perfect way to make a living—not cooped up in an office with someone looking over his shoulder. On the whole, passengers were friendly and orderly and the roads were well-maintained and generally uncongested. It was a peaceful way to earn an income. Maybe too peaceful, as lately Burl found himself falling asleep at the wheel. This wasn't necessarily a bad thing, he felt, except for the fact that in his dreams he kept colliding with an oncoming vehicle.

Parenting

His daughter died at a playground after falling from a set of monkey bars. He had told her to climb to the top. She was afraid but he felt she should confront her fears.

En Dessous de la Merde

After winning Olympic Gold in Paris in 1900 for his performance in underwater swimming, Charles de Vendeville spent the remainder of his days attempting to bring the sport back after it was dropped due to low spectator appeal. It was his contention that competitors could not be adequately seen swimming below the effluvia in the River Seine.

A Bolder Stand

My neighbor allows his dog to poop on my lawn and he doesn't pick it up. I haven't said anything to him, but it upsets me. I decide to put a friendly note in his mailbox rather than confront him in person, possibly causing a strain in our relationship, although I hardly know him because he's fairly new to the street. The next day I see he's allowing his mutt to shit on my lawn again, and I've had it. In the note I put in his mailbox this time, I withhold the word "Dear" in the salutation.

Discoveries Along State Highway 70

Granted, the Hotel Turkey in Turkey, Texas, doesn't look like much from the outside, but try its Trash Pizza ("Everything but the kitchen sink") and you'll be a lifelong fan.

Taking Action

The two nuns kept appearing at the events he attended—the ballgame, the movie, the outdoor concert. It seemed a weird coincidence, but he shrugged it off until he realized they were staring at him. He was tempted to confront them but resisted the urge, thinking he was being paranoid. However, when he found them standing on his lawn, he decided enough was enough. He would have to invite them in.

Guilty Pleasure

I'd been given the opportunity to go back in time and kill the baby Hitler. It was an honor to be chosen, and, of course, I took it. Yet, despite his being the monster he was, I'm haunted by the act of taking a life. My best friend, Benny Rosen, told me to get over it.

Tired of Her

His first wife was a year younger than he was but she'd died a decade ago. Meanwhile, he was in good health and living with his second wife. Recently his deceased ex appeared in his dreams almost nightly, and he found her more pleasing to be with than his current spouse. In his unconscious state, the woman he'd divorced after four years of marriage had grown into a more likeable and fun-loving individual, whose looks had also improved significantly. It wasn't lost on him that she now was the kind of woman he'd always wanted. He began to take frequent naps during the day hoping he'd encounter his former mate again, and this caught the attention of his extant partner, who found him growing more and more remote in his dealings with her. "What's the matter with you? You're not yourself," she complained. "All you want to do lately is sleep."

Suckle

She had many johns moan on her. Some shuddered as they did. *They are all little babies*, she told herself.

Inheritance

My grandma used to tell everyone I was the sweetest child in the world. I'm glad she died before people called me a menace to society for setting fire to my sister's house. She didn't deserve a bigger piece of my grandma's estate, because I remember her saying my sister was a silly little lady bug. In my mind, sweet trumps silly.

Less Than Reassuring Words from the IT Guy

"Sooner or later, in our techno-dependent world, things will stop working. What do you do when that happens? We haven't planned sufficiently for that inevitability. That's your post-apocalyptic world, my friend. Everything has a shelf-life."

A Very Different Kind of Day for Wilbur

He stood waiting at the end of his driveway for his ride into Hastings. He usually drove into town once a week for groceries and other necessities, but today he had to call a friend for a ride because his pickup wouldn't start. The sun felt unusually hot for late April, and he was feeling a little woozy. It was when he decided to sit down on an old rusty glide rocker left next to the road that he realized he wasn't where he thought he was. He wondered if a brain aneurysm was capable of transporting someone to the top of Disney's Twilight Zone Tower of Terror.

A Genius Solution

She could not get her iPhone facial recognition to work. "It's me!" she'd shout, each time she had to use her access code. Finally, she made an appointment with an Apple Store tech specialist and was told she should probably get a more recognizable face.

Curse of the Oscars

After watching *Nomadland*, he felt he'd found the answer to his predicament. He'd buy a used van with the few bucks he had left in his drained bank account and hit the road. Recently divorced and unemployed, there was nothing keeping him in Akron. If he stayed, he'd soon be homeless, he calculated. Within a week he was ready to set out. Purchasing a 1996 Dodge Grand Caravan with 87 thousand miles for $1,400 left him with $250, but he felt confident he was doing the right thing. That night he saw a story on national news reporting RV camp grounds around the country were filled to capacity with seniors trying to emulate Fern.

Not Everyone Has a Story Worth Telling

Marvin's been urged to write a memoir. He's resisted the notion, feeling that his past is not worthy of a book. "So, what if I had an encounter with the offspring of Godzilla?" he tells his friends. Only a handful agree.

Face Lift

While she was asleep, he removed her cherished beauty mark from her cheek and carefully wrapped it in a silk handkerchief. She felt nothing and didn't notice it was gone until late the next day. At first, she thought it must have come off on its own, and she searched in vain for it when she returned to her apartment after work. How the mole had suddenly disappeared confounded her. When she ran into her one night stand a few weeks later, she noticed something vaguely familiar about his appearance.

Colored Transportation

From Marvin's perspective, when you hit 76 you were just waiting for the death bus, and he was hoping there'd still be a seat left in the back.

Stored Away

The long-married couple were moved to a local assisted living facility. The wife had recently lost a leg to vascular disease and her husband was diagnosed with early stage dementia. Their daughter felt it was the best place for them. While she had a large home and therefore could easily accommodate them, she could not abide the notion of their living with her, even if it meant emptying her bank account to help pay for their care. The parents were thankful they had such a generous child. The last thing they wanted was to live with the person they still secretly referred to as that "little pain in the ass."

Getting it Right

According to a recent survey he'd come across, hamburgers were the most popular meal in America. It upset him that cheeseburgers came in second. He'd been wrong about a lot of things lately.

When the World Goes Strange at an Early Age

It wasn't until the end of the semester I noticed my history teacher's right forefinger was missing. I mentioned it to my classmates after school but they didn't believe me. It was too late to prove I was right, because we wouldn't be back in class until after the summer break. I thought maybe our art teacher, who lived two houses down from my family, could verify what I'd seen, and when I asked her, she said he certainly was lacking a finger, because she had it. "Would you like to see it?" she inquired.

Advantage, Jimmy.

When he almost drowned because some kid as a joke pulled him in over his head, he discovered he could remain submerged without air for an extremely long period. This gave him more than enough time to watch the kid drown who had pulled him under.

Across Time and Place

He hadn't seen his old flame in nearly 50 years, and now they were both elderly—in their mid-70s. He still recalled vividly their sexual liaisons at several motels within a short drive of their common workplace. Both married, they would engage in a frenzy of adulterous lovemaking during the stolen two or three-hour rendezvous. Now, she was in town for an appointment at Mass Eye and Ear, and they were to meet at her hotel. She had said nothing about her husband accompanying her.

Edit

I'm reviewing my manuscript and find it's quite wonderful until I'm halfway through. Then it seems to go flat and lose its luster. I read on and to my relief it appears to regain its power and originality in its last section. I figure I'll just delete its middle part but wonder if presses publish five page books.

Event Dying

Cy was bored with life. Old and infirm, little would lift his spirits. However, when he reminded himself he was close to the end, his mood improved. There would be something special to anticipate for however long it lasted.

Measure for Measure

He has his wife read everything he writes. She does so willingly and conscientiously, praising him when his stories deserve it but keeping her thoughts to herself when they don't. Her husband is especially sensitive to criticism about his writing. She's learned that the hard way. This time, however, she decides she can't keep her opinion to herself, because she's certain what her spouse has written is plagiarized. She believes it is an unconscious act so thinks he may not get so upset if she points it out. After all, it's not his writing, she tells herself.

What Scares the White People in Farm Country Iowa

Black women shaking their large, nearly bare posteriors to the primordial throb of Rakim on the *Grammys*. "I don't get those people," says Pa. His wife replies, "Awful," turning away from the screen in disgust.

Going to the Store for a Pack of Cigarettes

He could only catch part of his long-vanished father's coat sleeve as he rolled back the video. He'd freeze-framed it a dozen times hoping he'd see something he had missed, but nothing. It was always the same thing—his old man's arm resting on the sill of his car's open window as it slowly backed out of the driveway.

Michael C. Keith

There Are Limits to Everything

He'd developed the capacity to relax underwater without oxygen for an hour. Anything more stressed him.

Out of Sight, Out of Mind

He passed the hitchhiker at 7:30 in the morning on his way to
Dilley's Feed & Grain. He thought about giving the guy a lift
but figured he wasn't going far enough to make the ride
worthwhile to the traveler. *Can't be going to Dilley's,* he
reasoned, feeling guilty about leaving the stranger on a stretch
of the blacktop infamous for alien abductions. On his return
home, he'd forgotten he'd seen a hitchhiker.

Past-Imperfect

The fact that she's an *ex*-wife troubles her. There's nothing good about being an ex-wife, she concludes, so she begins to plot how she might get her ex-husband to remarry her, thus erasing the negative prefix. When she broaches the subject with him, he says he's had enough of her to last a lifetime and she'll have to adjust to the idea that she'll always be his *ex*-wife. She believes he's trying to suppress a chuckle and wonders if one remains an ex when one's ex is deceased.

What Do You Make of This?

Zero-point-three percent of the world's population has committed suicide. 99.7 percent stuck around.

Heartbreak in Ullapool

It had been 14 years since he left home and the woman he loved but couldn't have. He'd lost the two things dearest to him, and now he was returning. To his great relief, the town of his youth was how he'd remembered it, and he was thrilled to be back. Then he met up with his old flame, who'd just separated from the man who'd taken her from him. On seeing how she'd changed, he encouraged her to reconcile with his old rival.

Smart Technology

Bernice can't get the facial recognition to work on her iPhone after sleeping the night. She wonders why. When she reports it to Siri, the voice-controlled personal assistant calls her Pillow Head.

A Disappointing Return

Raoul passed his time in the ground thinking what it would be like when he'd be reanimated as he'd been promised by the holy man just before he succumbed. "You will breathe the air of this planet again," he was told. He hoped it would be somewhere other than Linfen . . . but it wasn't. Still, it was better than the airless box.

Coming to Terms with a Blue Desert

The ground surrounding their Mohave home was awash in a glow unlike anything they'd ever seen. "Weird sunrise," said Penelope, staring at the sliver of sun emerging on the distant horizon. "Never seen it that color before. It's pretty though." Her husband, Aiden, went into the yard for a closer look. "Man, that's not right," he reported, upon returning inside. "What's the matter, hon? You're scaring me." The kitchen window rattled as a sudden burst of wind slammed against it, causing Penelope to jump. "I think something really strange is happening," said Aiden, peering outside again. As if to corroborate his statement, the power went out and within seconds the house was bathed in a throbbing indigo light. At day's end, as they sat on the patio, they thought back at the strange experience that had interrupted their breakfast. "Guess we can reheat the bacon and eggs for supper," offered Penelope.

While Installing Power Lines in Big Bend National Park, He Observed

"There's a stretch we call rattlesnake run good for target practice and sharpening shooting skills. It gives us a clear view of the road and tourists in their cars. Some days we hit a few. Keeps us from going nuts out there."

Handy

After months of waiting patiently, something was finally sprouting where his severed thumb once was. His doctors had told him there were no guarantees when it came to limb regeneration, but they had seemed optimistic. It didn't matter to him that what was growing was a penis. In fact, the prospects excited him.

Sometimes You Want Something Too Much

When Burton was waiting for the advance copy of his first published book he feared something terrible would happen before it arrived, thus preventing him from ever seeing it. A day had not passed without his dreaming of having it in hand. It was the most exciting moment of his adult life. As the date of its arrival slowly approached he remained in his house and limited his activities, thereby thwarting the possibility of a deadly mishap. A few days before the scheduled delivery he camped out in his living room because of its close proximity to the front door where packages were left. When he received an email from Fed Ex indicating his package would arrive the next day, he held fast in his recliner, only leaving it to relieve himself. On the day of the big event he stopped going to the bathroom for fear he might have a fateful incident on the way. By the time the doorbell rang in the late afternoon, signaling the arrival of his author's copy, he'd become convinced it was a calculated attempt by dark forces to get him to fall and kill himself on the way to fetch his cherished self-published opus.

Thought Control

She was worried about taking a lie detector test. Not because she was guilty, but because she feared her mind would respond to questions in a way that would make her appear guilty.

Alternate Route

His car radio's on/off button was broken. At times, it would not turn on, and at other times it would not turn off. He was told by the dealer it would cost hundreds of dollars to correct because it was part of the vehicle's integrated control system––the FCIM assembly, so they said. Replacing it was the only way to address the problem. "Of course, you could just drive without sound," observed the service rep.

Avoiding the Hatchet

She asked if he was breaking up with her. He said, "What do you mean?" He'd have to carefully phrase his statement so that it was clear he was ending their relationship. How could he say it in a way that would not set her off? He'd seen what she'd done when her dog peed on the floor.

Surreal Safari

The wild life artist got the anatomies of the animals he painted on the Serengeti all wrong. They all had two legs, except for the giraffes, which had eight legs. The idea of a fifteen-foot tall creature with that many appendages freaked Bella out. Long-necked giant spiders were her worst nightmare.

#

What Do You Do with the Living Images of Your Dead Heroes on YouTube?

It excited and pleased her when she saw great writers and pop culture figures she admired in interviews and at events in old videos, but after a while it disturbed her that they'd long since passed away. She wondered if they got any pleasure at all in being viewed by future generations or if they felt it was a violation of their privacy.

Freedom from Pain

Iona was making an emergency visit to the dental clinic in Thornliebank to have a rotted tooth removed. When she arrived, she encountered a large crowd of protesters led by the First Minister of Scotland. *What an appropriate venue to make a stand for independence*, she thought.

Mentor

I'm reading the newest book by my favorite author, one who I attempt to emulate in my own writing. She has inspired many of my stories and greatly influenced my style. I have had some modest success finding small presses for my manuscripts, but I know I will never reach the heights she has attained with her work. She is revered and rightfully so. There are those days I question whether I should continue writing, since I know a contract from a large commercial publisher like hers is not in the cards for me. I wonder if she knew someone there.

We Are All Related in Our Need for Sugar

He spied a mouse on the kitchen floor eating a cookie crumb. He couldn't imagine killing something that also had a sweet tooth.

Sounds Like Death

There were no fourth floors in any of the buildings in the city of Padung, Indonesia. Now Lucas realized why it cost so little to buy three of them. He would never have purchased the 13th floor in buildings in the U.S, and he cursed his ignorance of southeast Asian culture and its shady realtors

Four Out of Five

Five people died in New York City on Christmas Day in 1930. The city's coroner speculated the deaths were likely related to recent events on Wall Street. One of the deceased was a seven-year-old girl.

Not What It Seemed

We saw the land for sale and were overwhelmed by its beauty. Magnificent green fields reaching out to smooth rolling hills. We could not imagine it could be ours for the price listed, so we quickly purchased it. Thankful such a magnificent place was now ours, we set out across its beckoning meadows with full hearts. It was when the ground under our feet sunk with our every step and burned the shoes off our feet we realized it was not such a bargain.

DIY Fail

He placed the wheelbarrow upright against the fence gate with the broken latch. It was his method for keeping out any would-be trespassers or unwelcome critters. When he found the wheelbarrow had been moved, he was at a loss as to what to do next.

Peenomenon

Aidan could hear conversation while he was urinating. Where it came from perplexed him because he was alone in his house. After he'd emptied his bladder, he looked out of the bathroom window and saw no one. Relieving himself a few hours later, he heard voices again. This time when he finished he did a thorough sweep of his house and the grounds surrounding it. Again, he encountered no one. It was during his 3 AM toilet run he discovered the source of the voices. How peculiar, he mused, that the contact of his urine with the commode porcelain would generate human discourse.

Revision

I look on the copyright page of the book I'm reading and learn that my literary role model is a few years younger than I am. Isn't it supposed to be the opposite, I think? I feel embarrassed I'm older than my mentor and decide to change the dedication in my forthcoming book.

No Further Explanation Required

"I was watching the news last night and it reported that this state has twice the number of missing persons as does the state with the second most missing persons. Why is that, you suppose?" asked Clay's friend.

"Well, it's *California*," he responded.

Michael C. Keith

Suicide

Dying on purpose.

Journal Entry

Just after my wife left the house to walk the dog I thought it might not be leashed properly and imagined it getting loose and running in front of a speeding car. This is the way my thoughts work lately, and they have not had a healthy effect on me.

They Don't Make It Easy

Alistair was stressed about his upcoming annual physical. He'd always experienced apprehension over medical exams (white coat anxiety, they called it), but it increased significantly when his doctor began giving him a memory test to detect early signs of dementia. "We do it for everyone once they hit 65," explained his long-time primary care physician. At first, he was relieved that it wasn't specific to him, but as his next yearly appointment approached, he began to obsess over it. *What if I get so nervous I freeze and can't give the correct answers. Will I be wrongly diagnosed with the disease?* he fretted. When he narrowly passed the mental quiz, he decided to immediately prepare for the next one. It upset him his doctor would not provide him with a study guide.

It Was Something John Prine Said

"I like his quote about cereal. You know the one, 'I was staring at my oatmeal 'til I got cross-eyed.' Believe that was it. Close anyway. There's a lot there if you think about it."

The Desperation in Things Running Out

Our food supply is getting low. The refrigerator and cupboards are looking bare. There's not any milk for our coffee, and tonight it looks like beans and potatoes for supper. We have to go grocery shopping, but the prospect makes us anxious. The virus is still lurking. Better to starve than go out where it's not safe, we think.

A Leg Up

She once was a beauty, and now at 80 she'd lost most of it. But what she had left still kept her more beautiful than all of her 80-year-old friends, and she took pleasure in that.

On What Planet Did That Happen?

Aileen refused to pay for an operation that only made matters worse. It made no sense to her to be charged for a procedure that had failed. If fact, she believed the hospital should compensate her for the greater discomfort she now experienced. They agreed completely and returned what they'd charged for the surgery, plus a not insubstantial sum for any inconvenience it had caused her.

Beautiful Noise

I don't mind my tinnitus anymore. In fact, I'd hate to be without it. At the beginning, I found it distracting but eventually discovered I can shape it into any sound I like. Imagine the pleasure I get hearing the Hotsy-Totsy Boys whenever I want.

Revisiting the Scene of the Crime

I go to the Ford dealer due to a recurring issue with my car's in-dash computer. I'm really peeved. This has cost me a lot of time and money, I complain to the service rep. "Yeah, these damn cars are nothing but trouble when they get a couple of years on them," he says, and follows his comment with a suggestion I buy a *new* Ford.

His Golden Years

Finn was calculating how long he could live on what he'd saved for retirement in combination with his monthly Social Security check. He was 66 and thought he had another 20 years ahead of him. After doing the math, it appeared he'd run out of his 401K four years before his projected demise, leaving him with only his paltry government stipend to get him by on. How to survive his remaining time on the planet became an all-consuming question. When he told his best friend about his dilemma, he was provided with a possible solution, although he was not sure he would have the courage to drive off a cliff on his 82nd birthday.

Dry Night

He knew if he reached orgasm with the stranger in his dream, the relationship with his wife would be over, so he woke himself up just in time to save his marriage.

Hobby Boys

Archie's collection of in-flight sickness bags kept him going during the pandemic. In that time, he'd amassed an additional two hundred regurgitation pouches to include in his ever-expanding archive. He knew people thought his avocation strange, but he felt it was nowhere near as odd as his best friend's obsession with Japanese beetle fighting. When they got together their conversation often centered on their inability to find dates.

A Good Beef

Harlan chose filet mignon and potatoes au gratin for his last meal the night of his execution. He was told his selection was not possible but a hamburger and fries could be substituted. "It's my right to have the meal I want!" he angrily protested. In response to his impertinence, the warden sentenced him to 30 days in solitary confinement.

Fact

Most people die feeling lousy.

The Strangers Next Door

Our neighbors have gone cold on us. No more friendly waves or chitchats. We're vexed and disturbed by the sudden silence and attempt to find out why the snub, but our calls go unanswered. We've noticed ambulances going down our street late at night and wonder if there's something going on we don't know about. Finally, we decide to confront the situation head on and go to our neighbor's houses, but no one answers their door. My wife thinks she might know what the problem is, but I don't think it has anything to do with the blood stains on our clothes.

Atlas Shrugged

"Nobody talks about geography anymore. When we were kids we would play U. S. Capitols. You know, name the capitol of a state. Whoever came up with it first won. I was really good at it because I studied my Rand McNally. Now people, especially kids, couldn't tell you the capitol of Manitoba."

The Value of Life Work

He'd spent his career studying water scorpions only to conclude they were poor swimmers. He wondered if his research made a genuine contribution to the field arachnology.

Little Laurie, 9:30

The pink tricycle lay on its side in the street.

Last Wish 2

Most people don't want to die alone, but Sidney was an exception. He felt passing in front of loved ones was embarrassing. *Who wants to be seen at the most vulnerable and depleted moment in one's life?* he thought, and forbade any living thing be in his presence as he succumbed. With his last breath, he ordered his dog from the room.

Word Power

Mateo wasn't teased about his last name until his classmates reached a higher level of literacy. It was then Penes became Penis.

Reassessment

It was his best painting ever, or so he felt. He had never received such praise for his compositions as he had for it, and he felt he'd achieved something extraordinary. As the weeks passed, his confidence in its quality diminished. Ultimately, he could not look at the abstract without feeling he'd failed. Disheartened, he placed the canvas in a dark corner of his studio and forgot about it, until it was purchased for the highest price ever paid for one of his art works. "You've acquired my finest painting," he confided to his patron.

Saint Arlene

Her rheumatoid arthritis was first diagnosed when she was a freshman in high school. By the time she was 30, her gnarled body was confined to a wheel chair. From it she would wish everyone a wonderful day.

Home Invaders

We have squirrels in the attic and between the walls of our old house. Their noisy activity keeps us awake at night. We call for assistance and are told the pests will need to be trapped, removed, and released. The animal control professional adds, "Of course, they'll just come back." We pay for his services and for the one night of uninterrupted sleep that follows.

If Wishes Were Horses

He ate a cube of butter. It was the only thing remaining of the provisions left for him. *If I only had a nice loaf of French bread*, he thought.

"The Bigger the Man, the Deeper the Imprint"

My father was older than John Wayne, and in his mind, that gave him something over the Duke. When I'd remind him he was two-and-a-half years senior to the famous screen hero, a look of satisfaction would come over him and he would swagger across the kitchen to the refrigerator for another Coors Lite.

The Burden of Longevity

At 83-years-old, Shamus had not experienced a death in his family or among his friends. In fact, everyone he knew, including his great-grandparents, was in robust health. This put him in a gloomy state of mind. *I probably won't die either,* he told himself,

A Dietary Approach

I never could get my alcoholic, chain-smoking father to eat what was on his plate. Food meant little to him. We'd cook a nice meal, and he'd take a couple of bites, push his plate away, and go out on the porch for a cigarette. It frustrated my wife, but I knew the best thing to feed him was half of a plain cheese sandwich. That he generally finished.

News Spreads

The trees along the path he regularly walked had changed location. When he reported it to the town constable, he was told he was not the first to provide him with that information.

Old Mr. Murphy's Rant

"People call convenience stores variety stores, but they're wrong to do that. Variety stores sell general merchandise, like hardware, clothes, auto parts, and so-forth. Sure, they sell groceries, too, but that's mainly what convenience stores do. You won't find coveralls or wrenches in them. I hate when people get things like that wrong. People are careless with their statements. There's too much erroneous information in the world already."

Inconvenienced

We had plans to travel to Atlanta to visit my wife's aunt but the day before our flight we were informed she had passed away. This leaves a substantial gap in our schedule not easily filled. We would hope she'd realize this were she still alive.

Terror Firma

In her dreams, she fell from great heights waking up just before hitting the ground. She was told if she'd landed she would die.

Powers Beyond

There wasn't a single point of light along Ginger Street. It was as dark as nine-year-old Maggie had ever experienced on her walk home from her aunt's house. The power had gone out in the neighborhood just after sunset, and before she was stuck staying the night away from her own room, she'd made a dash for it. She knew it wasn't the smartest thing to do with reports of an escaped circus lion in the vicinity, but she couldn't imagine being in any danger with the rabbit's foot her father had given her the day after he'd died. "Wave the amulet in front of anything wishing you ill," he'd told her. She clutched it as she once had his hand.

Her Wheel of Fortune

She occasionally solved the puzzle with one letter. Frequently solved the puzzle with two letters. Always solved the puzzle with three letters.

Fair Warning

With the government's recent acknowledgement of the existence of UFOs, Char felt relieved. He'd taken so much flack for arguing that Earth had been visited by aliens he was tempted to throw in the towel and return to his home planet. Now, he felt humans were ready for Phase Two.

Diminishing Returns

He was down to about one-tenth of the sensation he'd previously felt during orgasm. *That's ten percent a decade since I was born*, he calculated.

What Came Next for Her

It wasn't the first time a relationship in her life had failed, but it was the most devastating. She'd never loved anyone like she had him. Now she was left to deal with her shattered emotions and she had doubts she could. It felt that devastating to her. Just as things seemed at their darkest, she was informed her ex-boyfriend had proposed to her step-sister. The one she couldn't stand. The one she wanted to kill. Sure, she would be happy to serve as her bridesmaid.

Cosmic Mystery

Despite extensive investigation by medical researchers, it was not determined why captured aliens excreted in primary colors.

Relative Safety

She thought if she had to—that is, if she were threatened and had to protect her life—she could put some poison in her fried chicken. Everybody loved her family recipe, and no one would turn it down. It was famous throughout the county. So there was no one she couldn't lay low if she had to. Just give whoever was intending to do her harm a leg or thigh, and that would take care of the problem. She owed her great grandma's cooking for her peace of mind.

The Salvation in Vicarious Travel

It's raining hard as I sit before my computer in the grey minutes before dawn. I'm not sure I can make it through the day ahead. The challenge seems beyond me. Sunny beaches on YouTube no longer help.

Differing Opinions

He believed the world was permanently altered in 2020. Whack job president, the pandemic, gun violence, and climate change headed his list of reasons. I said I thought the current year was worse with the asteroid scheduled to hit Earth and devastate the planet. He said no, I should review 2020.

Michael C. Keith

Marcel's Way

"Can you imagine?" asked my literary friend, "Proust would orgasm while observing two famished rats attacking one another. The more violent the battle between the rodents the greater the arc of his ejaculate."

Dower Dougher

Marlene was brilliant when it came to baking Gloucester bread. People came from far off to buy loaves and many went away empty handed because of how quickly they sold out. Customers often became angry when they couldn't get any and on more than one occasion she was asked why she didn't make more to accommodate the demand. "I'm not a bread making machine, you know," she would answer.

There Are Hardships in the World

The cantata performed by the conifers in the upper forest kept the people in the city awake long after their usual bedtime.

Something Lost

I hardly ever talk to anyone on the phone. If I want to say something to someone, I email or text them. Then when I see them we're awkward with one another, almost like strangers. It's an inconvenience, but I think maybe we should message with our voices more often.

Lowered Education

Professor Pierce wasn't sure he was fully qualified to teach college students. He felt his knowledge of his subject was thin, if not superficial, and that he essentially taught the Cliff Notes version of his discipline to get through the semester. Consequently, he viewed himself as a bit of a fraud, although his student course evaluations were always among the highest in his department. Bringing cookies and pizza to class had been one of his better ideas.

Existential Questions

You witness your loved one being shot. The killer runs and you pursue him. Should you not be comforting the dying? What does this say about you?

Oh, What a Beautiful Morning

We travel well together, except when I've been driving all day. Then I become grumpy and snap at her. She takes offense and says we should fly the next time. I remind her she hates to fly. We reach the motel and watch an episode of Ken Burns' documentary on the national park system in silence. When we set out on the road the next day, we're all smiles.

Why Me?

The power has been out at his house but not at his neighbors. He feels singled out and then he realizes he hasn't paid his bill. He pays it immediately but still has no power. Again, he feels singled out.

Friends with No Benefits

I checked out his wheelhouse when he wasn't there. It surprised me how empty it was. Barren, you might say. He was so secretive about his wheelhouse I thought something of real value must be there. You know how disappointing it is when you discover someone you thought had a lot in his wheelhouse really has nothing there?

Future of the Book

Bella believed the one remaining press in the country would select her first novel as their single publication for the year. *They don't actually read submissions,* she reassured herself.

ABOUT THE AUTHOR

Michael C. Keith is the author or coauthor of more than two dozen groundbreaking books on electronic media, including one chosen by President Clinton for his official summer reading list. Beyond that, he is the author of an acclaimed memoir (*The Next Better Place*, Algonquin Books), a young adult novel, and 19 story collections—his latest *Insomnia 11* from MadHat Press and *Pieces of Bones and Rags* from Cabal Books. He has received accolades for his academic and fiction writing.

CPSIA information can be obtained
at www.ICGtesting.com
Printed in the USA
JSHW021940270622
27451JS00001B/55